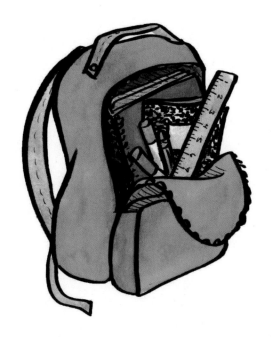

THIS BOOK BELONGS TO:

_____

One of the best parts of being a BIG kid is going to KINDERGARTEN. It's a fun and exciting time. And there are so many things you can do so you're prepared!

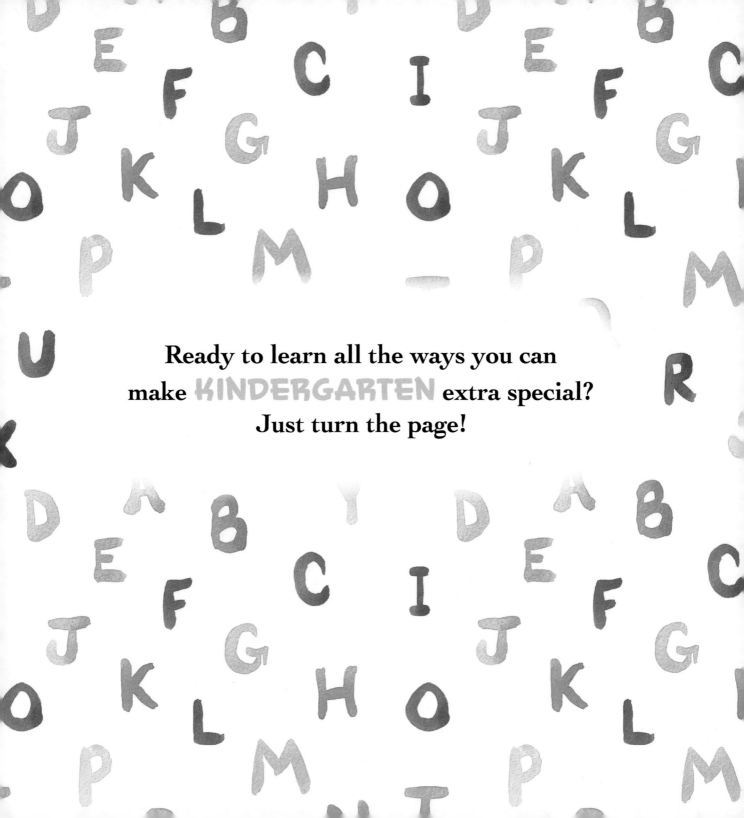

Ready to learn all the ways you can make **KINDERGARTEN** extra special? Just turn the page!

The night before **KINDERGARTEN** is a great time to pack your supplies. What will you put into your backpack?

Once you're packed and ready, it's time to get in bed.
A good night's sleep will help you feel
rested and ready for the day ahead.

Wake up!
The big day is finally here.

Get dressed and ready.

Eat a healthy breakfast.

Off to **KINDERGARTEN** you go!

KINDERGARTEN is fun and exciting, but it is also something new.

And sometimes, new things can be scary.

Just remember . . . you're not the only one who might feel scared.

KINDERGARTEN is a new experience for everyone.

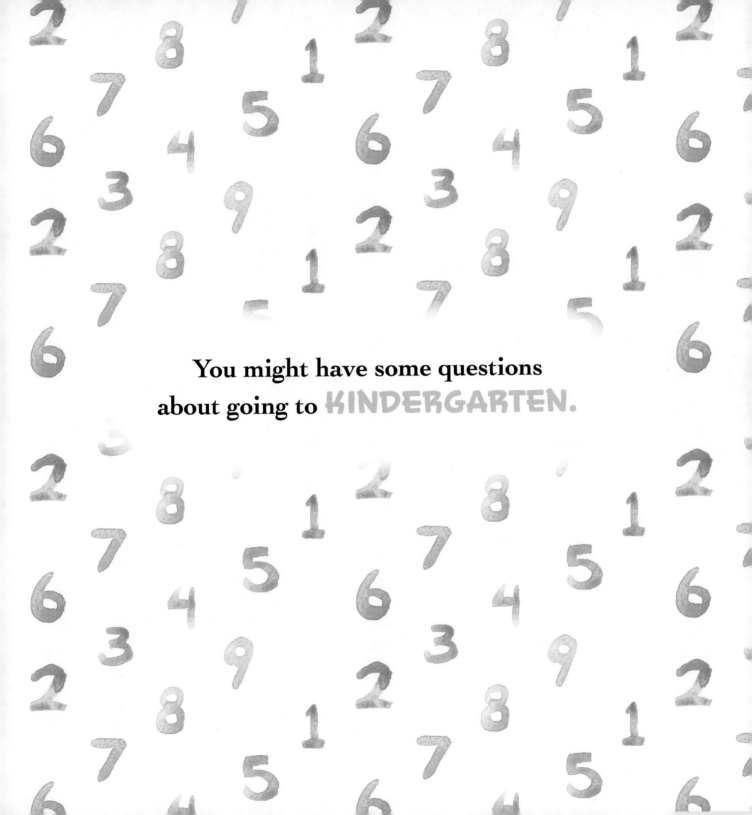

You might have some questions
about going to **KINDERGARTEN.**

Your teacher has been waiting all summer for **KINDERGARTEN** to begin and can't wait to meet all of the new students. When you arrive, just remember to be polite and respectful.

**There's a simple trick to making friends.
All you have to do is treat others
how you want them to treat you.**

There are so many good ways to show other kids that you want to be their friend.

PLAY
LAUGH
TALK
SHARE

LISTEN

GREET

SMILE

HELP

There are so many fun things you will learn and do in KINDERGARTEN.

You will learn about letters and numbers.

You will read books and share stories.

You will draw, color, and paint.

You will jump.

You will run.

You will sing.

You will dance.

You will have lots
of time to play!

Before you know it, the day will be over
and your family will be waiting for you.

They will be so excited to hear
all about KINDERGARTEN...